Kitty's magic

Shadow the Lonely Cat

Ella Moonheart

BLOOMSBURY

LONDON OXFORD NEW YORK NEW DELHI SYDNEY

Chapter 1

Kitty Kimura rushed out of the school gates with her best friend, Jenny. 'Grandma said she'll be picking us up today,' called Kitty. 'Look, there she is!'

Kitty's grandmother was waiting for the girls with a smile on her face. Grandma was Japanese and, like her eight-year-old granddaughter, she had almond-shaped eyes and shiny black hair – but Grandma's bob had a pure white streak running through it. She lived with Kitty and her parents, who ran a special shop selling Japanese gifts. It was Grandma who had given Kitty her nickname. Kitty's *real* name was Koemi, but hardly anybody called her that.

'Hello, girls!' Grandma said. 'How was school today?'

As they walked home, Kitty and Jenny told Grandma their news.

'Our teacher Ms Brookes says we're starting a special project soon, where we do something to help the community,' Kitty explained. 'Every year her class does something different. Last year they picked up litter in the park.'

'We all have to think of ideas and give them to Ms Brookes,' added Jenny. 'Then she'll pick the best one.'

'I'm sure you girls will think of something,' Grandma told them.

'Kitty, why don't you come over to my house this week?' Jenny said. 'We could try to think of an idea then, and play with Misty!' Misty was Jenny's cat, a pretty silver tabby with blue eyes.

'Good idea!' Kitty told her friend, grinning.

Jenny continued chatting excitedly, describing how cute it was when Misty leapt at the point of light from the new laser pen she'd got. But what Jenny didn't realise was that Kitty already knew about it. Someone else had told her the night before: Misty herself!

Kitty had a *very* special secret.

Just a few weeks ago, Kitty had discovered something amazing about herself. She'd always believed she was allergic to cats, but one day Grandma had given her an unusual present: a beautiful necklace with a silver pendant, engraved with some mysterious words.

That night, Kitty had gone to a sleep-over at Jenny's house. When Jenny was fast asleep, with Misty curled up close by, Kitty had sneezed an especially powerful sneeze. When she opened her eyes, she was no longer a girl – she had turned into a cat!

Even better, she learned that all cats could talk to each other. Misty had quickly become her very best cat friend, and Kitty was getting to know lots of other cats in town too. She was still getting used to her incredible gift. It turned out that the special words written on her necklace could help Kitty control when she turned into a cat, if she needed to. Kitty knew she had to be careful that nobody else knew about her ability, because if her secret got out, the magic would be broken forever.

Kitty and Jenny skipped ahead of Grandma, but as they turned the next corner, Kitty realised her friend was slowing down. 'What's wrong?' she asked.

Jenny pointed up ahead of them. 'Mrs Thornton's house is so spooky,' she said.

Kitty looked up the path lined with crooked old trees that led up to a big house at the top of a small, steep hill. The garden had a huge tree with twisted branches. It was full of tall, tangled, overgrown weeds, the black paint on the front door was peeling, and three of the windows were cracked. 'I know!' Kitty replied, shivering. 'My mum says she used to see Mrs Thornton doing shopping in town, but no one's seen her around recently. She's really old.'

'Some of the kids in our class say she's a witch,' added Jenny, eyeing the house nervously. 'She has a black cat

called Shadow, and they say he's a witch's cat. Look — he's over there!'

Kitty caught a glimpse of wild dark fur and glinting eyes among the weeds. Shadow was crouched low, and Kitty could only just make him out. She remembered having met him once, but during all the nights she'd spent wandering around town in her cat form, she hadn't bumped into Shadow since.

She tried to call him over, but Shadow turned away, darting through the bushes. Kitty saw the broken cat flap on the front door swinging as he rushed inside. *He obviously wants to stay close to home,* she thought.

After Kitty and Grandma had dropped Jenny off at home and walked along the street to their own house, Kitty decided to ask Grandma if she knew why she hadn't seen Shadow lately. After all, she was the perfect person to ask about any cat in town – because Kitty wasn't the only human who could turn into a cat. Grandma had the very same gift!

'Grandma, do you know anything about Shadow, the black cat who lives with Mrs Thornton?' she asked.

Grandma paused. 'Shadow?' she said. 'Let me think. He used to come to our Cat Council meetings all the time, but recently he's been keeping to himself. He tends to stay in his own house or garden.'

The Cat Council was a special

gathering of cats from all over town, which met at night and helped cats with their problems. Kitty and Misty were the newest members of the Cat Council, and Kitty had an extra-special role. She had been chosen to take over from Grandma as the Guardian, the leader of the Council! Kitty was very proud to be the Guardian, and had promised to do the best job she could. 'So Shadow hasn't always been like this?' she said.

Grandma glanced at Kitty and smiled. 'Why are you asking, Kitty?' she said.

Kitty nodded. 'There must be a reason for Shadow behaving differently,' she said. 'Maybe he needs some help?'

Chapter 2

After dinner that evening, Kitty's mum explained that she and Dad were travelling to Manchester the next morning, to visit a special fair selling Japanese objects. They were hoping to find some unusual ornaments to stock in their shop.

Mrs Kimura bent down to give Kitty a goodnight kiss. 'Grandma will take you to school and pick you up, OK, sweetheart?'

'OK!' replied Kitty, trying not to sound too eager. Once her parents had gone to bed, Kitty knew that she would be free to change into a cat, without risking being seen. Then she could start finding out what was going on with Shadow, and whether she could help.

Kitty waited for her parents' bedroom door to close, and then counted to a hundred. Soon everything was still, and she was sure that they must have fallen asleep. As quietly as she could, Kitty opened her bedroom window, and then very quietly, she whispered the words that were also etched on to the pendant on her necklace.

'Human hands to kitten paws,
Human fingers, kitten claws.'

Straight away, the strange, fizzing, tickling feeling began. Kitty grinned as an incredible tingly feeling swept through her feet and legs, then her tummy and arms, right up to the top of her head and the tips of her fingers. She closed her eyes and waited for the feeling to stop, took a deep breath and opened her eyes.

Kitty always thought it was funny how much bigger her cosy little bedroom seemed once she was in her cat form. Her bed towered above her, and her animal posters and photographs of Jenny and Misty seemed miles away. She lifted a fuzzy black front leg, and giggled to see a small, furry white-tipped paw with tiny claws. She let out an excited little mew, and looked back to see her long, furry tail swish behind her. She shook out her whiskers and trotted around the rug on her bedroom floor, thrilled to be back in her cat form. *This is so amazing*, she thought to herself. *I'm not sure I'll ever get used to it!*

Kitty crouched low against the carpet, then sprang into the air, landing lightly on the window sill. She caught sight of her reflection in the window: a small black face with neat little ears, bright green eyes, a pink nose and whiskers. Round her neck was a collar with a silver pendant. Kitty's necklace also changed when she became a cat!

She breathed in the amazing mixture of smells from the garden: freshly cut grass, flowers, Grandma's herb patch, and the scent of several cats, including Misty's and her own. Kitty's sense of smell was much stronger when she turned into a cat – and so was her ability to see in the dark. It was one of the things she loved best about her gift.

With a little wriggle, she crouched low, then used her strong back legs to jump straight out of the window. She landed on the kitchen roof, then leapt the rest of the way into the garden. She trotted through the grass, getting used to working her four furry little legs together now, sprang up on to the roof of her Wendy house, then hopped on to the garden fence. With her tail arched for extra balance, and her claws gripping the wood, she could run along easily. And Kitty knew exactly where she wanted to head first: Shadow's house.

It was dark now though, and as she neared Mrs Thornton's house, the path grew very quiet. Although Kitty's sharp eyes could see in the gloom, she still felt a little bit nervous. *I wish I'd asked Misty to come along*, she thought, as her heartbeat started to quicken.

Kitty padded slowly up to the front gate and peered through it. She could just make out the gleam of a pair of eyes, and realised that Shadow was crouched on the steps in front of the door. Kitty miaowed to say hello. 'My name's Kitty,' she said, as cheerfully as she could manage. 'I think we met at the Cat Council once, but I don't think I've seen you there lately. Is everything all right?'

There was a silence, then Kitty heard a low growl. She had already learned that this was a very unfriendly noise for cats to make, and hesitated. Should she try again?

'It must be a bit quiet living all the way up here, away from the town

without any other cats to talk to. Maybe if you came out to –' Kitty began, but she jumped as Shadow's growl became a nasty hiss.

'No!' he miaowed quickly. 'I'm not leaving my garden again.'

Kitty frowned. What did that mean? Why was Shadow being so unfriendly? She trotted away from his house a little, not sure what to do. Then Kitty spotted three small scratch marks in a tree trunk close by. They made a triangle shape, and she knew this mark was important. It was the sign that another neighbourhood cat had called a meeting of the Cat Council. Someone else might need her help!

Suddenly, in the distance, Kitty heard

several cats miaowing a special call out into the night air. They were all voices she recognised as being part of the Cat Council. The meeting was about to start!

'Listen,' she said, turning and trotting back the way she came. 'I'm going to the Cat Council meeting right now.

Why don't you come along? It's a lovely warm night. You could stretch your legs and –'

'Go away!' said Shadow. 'I'm staying right here!'

Kitty decided it was better not to make Shadow even more upset or angry for now. She turned and trotted back down the hill, heading in the direction of the woods where the Cat Council always met. *I'll leave Shadow alone for the moment*, she thought. *But hopefully I'll be able to find out what's wrong soon. I just need to figure out a way to get him to talk to me!*

Chapter 3

Kitty ran through the dark wood and headed towards the clearing, where a group of cats were gathering together in a circle. Kitty spotted Tiger, the rather bossy but kind old tomcat who led the Cat Council, perched in between a glamorous British Shorthair called Coco and a friendly grey cat named Smoky. Other cats were still arriving from all directions, miaowing hello and trotting to their places.

'Hi, Kitty!' called Misty as Kitty padded up to the circle. Kitty miaowed a greeting to everyone, and said hello to those nearby, including her friend, by gently bumping heads with them. Then Kitty trotted to her place next to a small black cat with a white patch on her head – Grandma in her cat form!

'I think that's everyone tonight! Let's start by saying the Miaow Vow,' suggested Tiger.

Together, the cats recited the special words that started every meeting of the Cat Council:

We promise now,
This solemn vow,

To help somehow,
When you miaow.'

Tiger nodded once the Vow was finished. 'Now, which cat called today's meeting?' he asked, looking round.

A fluffy young tortoiseshell stepped into the circle. Kitty noticed she was walking with a slight limp, placing one paw down on the ground very carefully. 'My name is Bella,' the cat introduced herself.

'Welcome, Bella,' replied Tiger. 'Do you have a problem to share with us? Kitty here is going to be taking over as our Guardian. She might be able to give you some advice.' He gestured with a paw to show Bella where Kitty was sitting.

Kitty nodded at Bella, hoping that she'd be able to help. 'Yes! Tell us what the problem is, and I'll definitely do my best,' she miaowed warmly. She knew how coming to the Cat Council for the first time could make a cat feel nervous, and tried her best to make new cats feel at ease. It wasn't so long ago that she was new too!

'Well, I'm having problems with my human, Max,' Bella explained.

'Is he unkind to you?' asked a little white kitten named Poppy, blinking worriedly.

'No, Max is a lovely human,' replied Bella. 'But recently, he's been putting these funny white things in my food! They're small and round, a bit like tiny pebbles. They taste funny too. I want to ask you all, how I can avoid eating them?'

Kitty giggled to herself. She knew exactly what the white things must be – medicine! She had watched a programme about vets and had seen them doing the exact same thing, hiding pills inside bowls of animals' food.

But the rest of the Council had a very different reaction to Bella's story – and before Kitty could say anything, they were all giving Bella their own suggestions! 'You must do everything you can not to eat the pebbles!' announced Tiger loudly. 'Hide them under your paws until your human goes away. Then push them under the sofa or the doormat – somewhere he won't notice them!'

'Or you could *pretend* to eat them,' added Smoky seriously. 'Keep them hidden in your cheek and then spit them out when Max isn't looking.'

'Just refuse,' said Coco airily. 'My human can never force me to do anything I don't want to. She knows I'm the boss in our house! If I were you, Bella, I would simply hiss and spit until your human stops putting the nasty things in your bowl. That ought to do the trick!'

Kitty decided it was time to jump in. 'Bella, I think you *should* eat them,' she said.

The other cats turned to look at her.

'What do you mean?' asked Bella, puzzled, but Grandma nodded encouragingly at Kitty.

'They're not pebbles, you see. They're medicine,' explained Kitty. 'Special things to make you better, when you're poorly. Have you felt poorly recently, Bella?'

Bella cocked her head to one side thoughtfully. 'Well, I *do* have a sore paw,' she admitted. 'I scratched it on a thorn in the garden. It's very painful, and I've been limping ever since!'

'I think Max is giving you medicine to help your paw heal,' Kitty told her.

'It might not taste very nice, but I promise that he wouldn't add it to your food unless you really needed it. You won't have to take them for long – just until your paw feels better.'

There was a murmur around the circle, and Bella looked impressed. 'Gosh, I had no idea!' she miaowed. 'Well, I'll give it a try. Thank you.'

Grandma gave a proud purr.

'Well done, Kitty!' Misty said. 'None of us normal cats would have known that.'

'That's right! Because you're human too, you've got all sorts of extra knowledge to help us cats out,' added Smoky. 'That's what makes you such a good Guardian!'

Kitty purred happily as the rest of

the Council nodded. She always felt happy when she was able to solve a problem for one of her new cat friends.

'Now, does anyone have any other problems they need help with?' asked Tiger, looking round the circle.

Kitty stepped forward. 'Actually, I wanted to ask you all about a cat called Shadow,' she miaowed. 'I'm sure lots of you know him, but he hasn't come to a Council meeting for a long time. In fact, he refuses to leave his garden. I want to see if I can get Shadow to tell me what's wrong.'

The rest of the Council hesitated. 'I don't think there's anything *wrong* with Shadow. He just seems old and grumpy to me,' Coco said, licking a paw.

Kitty couldn't argue with that. He did seem a bit moody. 'Does anyone know if he's had any problems recently?'

The cats looked at one another, shaking their heads.

'I knew Shadow when we were both kittens, no bigger than young Poppy here,' said Pinky, an old Sphynx cat. Kitty always thought Pinky was really interesting, because she was a type of cat that didn't have any fur! 'He used to be a friendly cat,' Pinky continued. 'He'd play with the leaves in the park with us, he'd help us chase away that nasty fox that used to lurk around the town centre … But lately he refuses to leave his human's garden.'

Kitty frowned. 'I wonder what changed?'

'Shadow's scary!' piped up little Poppy, shivering. 'I went exploring near his house one day. It's creepy, and he just seems to hide in the dark up there.'

Kitty agreed that it was a bit gloomy and overgrown up at Shadow's house. She'd felt a bit nervous there herself. But that didn't mean they shouldn't try to help him, did it?

But the other cats didn't seem to think it was worth it. 'I think it's best to leave Shadow alone,' Tiger said to the group. 'It seems to me like he prefers being by himself.'

Soon after that, Tiger announced that the meeting was over. Kitty felt disappointed. Something must have happened to make Shadow change. Even if he didn't want to come out and play with the other cats, surely they should try to get to the bottom of why he was behaving in such an unfriendly way? Kitty was new to being the Guardian, but she was certain that she should try to do something. There was a cat that needed her help!

Chapter 4

The next day, Kitty went to Jenny's house after school. 'We can play with Misty and the laser pen!' Jenny said as they dropped their school bags by the front door. 'Let's go and find her.'

Misty was curled up in the sunshine on the kitchen window sill, and jumped straight down with a happy miaow when she saw the girls come in. Jenny found the laser pen and switched it on, pointing the beam at the wall. Kitty giggled as Misty leapt at it, swiping the tiny circle of light excitedly with her paws. Jenny waved the pen around the kitchen and Misty darted under chairs as she chased the light. 'See, she loves it!' exclaimed Jenny.

Kitty grinned, remembering how excited Misty had been when she described the game. When Jenny went to answer the phone in the hallway, Kitty crouched down and whispered to Misty, 'That does look like a lot of fun! Sometimes I wish I had my own human to play with when I turn into a cat – then I'd be able to join in games like that too!'

Misty purred in agreement and rubbed her furry head against Kitty's ankles. Kitty knew that Misty could still understand everything she said, like all cats could understand humans. Kitty could only understand Misty's cat sounds when she was a cat herself, though.

As Jenny came back into the kitchen, Kitty quickly stopped talking.

'That was your grandma on the phone! She says your dinner's ready,' Jenny explained. 'See you at school tomorrow? Maybe we'll come up with a good idea for our community project then. I still haven't thought of anything!'

Kitty ate her spaghetti very quickly – so quickly that Grandma chuckled as she took her last bite. 'You're in a hurry tonight, Kitty!' she said, smiling. 'I bet I can guess why.'

Kitty grinned. 'I want to change into a cat again this evening!' she explained. 'I thought with Mum and Dad still being away I could use the chance to go out a bit earlier. Would that be OK?'

'I don't see why not,' Grandma told her. 'Just be careful while you're out and about.'

'I will,' promised Kitty, and then she remembered something. 'Grandma, I was thinking about Shadow. It seems a shame that nobody at the Cat Council wanted to find out why he won't come out of his garden, don't you think? I know he's a bit grumpy, but maybe he's unhappy. I really want to think of a way to help him.'

Grandma smiled at Kitty. 'That, my dear, is why you will make such a wonderful Guardian,' she said. 'You're always looking to help. I'm sure you'll figure out if there's anything you can help him with soon enough.' Grandma gave Kitty's hand a squeeze.

Kitty quickly put her plate in the sink and slipped out into the garden. This was a safe place to change into a cat, because it was sheltered from all the neighbouring houses by tall trees and bushes. Quietly, she spoke the words she needed to change form, and closed her eyes as the bubbling, fizzing feeling swept through her. It was so fantastic, every time!

When she opened her eyes again, every blade of grass around her seemed clearer and greener, and she could hear the sound of a tiny butterfly fluttering its wings right at the other end of the garden. She gave a happy miaow, and flexed her tail. She paused to give her white-tipped paws and legs a quick clean, swiping her paws over her quivering whiskers quickly too. She was still getting used to having all that soft, fuzzy black fur!

Kitty's cat ears pricked up as the back door opened behind her, and

Grandma stepped outside. She bent down to give Kitty's head a gentle stroke and tickle the fur on her back.

'Have fun!' Grandma whispered.

Kitty purred happily, then jumped up on to the garden fence and trotted along it until she reached the street. It was a lovely summer evening and Kitty enjoyed being in cat form while it was still a little bit light outside.

As she padded along, past Jenny's house and around the next corner, she caught a glimpse of tortoiseshell fur ahead of her. The cat turned and Kitty realised it was Bella, the young cat who had come to the Cat Council meeting and asked about the little white pills her human was hiding in her food bowl.

'Bella!' miaowed Kitty, and the two cats bumped their foreheads together in a friendly greeting.

'I ate my medicine up today, just like you said,' Bella told Kitty proudly. 'And my poorly paw is already feeling lots better! So I've come out to play! Let's go and see if we can find a mouse to catch!' the little cat suggested eagerly, giving an excited leap and then racing off down the street.

Kitty wasn't sure she liked that idea very much. The thought of it made her tummy feel a bit funny! Even so, she ran after Bella and quickly caught up. As the cats began to trot down the next street, Kitty suddenly felt an odd prickling feeling along her back. Without even

meaning to, she had pricked up her ears
and was crouching close to the ground.
Bella was doing the same, and letting out
a low growl.

What's going on? Kitty wondered, glancing around.

Suddenly she spotted what was making her behave so strangely. Walking down the street from the other direction was a young man and his fierce-looking Alsatian dog!

The dog narrowed his mean black eyes as he spotted the cats. He lurched straight forward, pulling hard on his lead, and the man had to struggle to keep hold of the other end. 'Nipper, stop it!' he shouted.

The dog took no notice, but opened his mouth and began to bark loudly, revealing a glimpse of sharp white teeth. As he pulled forward, the young man began to stumble and dropped the lead. Bella let out a frightened hiss and darted away, but Kitty felt frozen to the spot. She stared in horror as the Alsatian broke free and began thundering down the street, heading straight towards her!

Chapter 5

As the growling dog ran towards Kitty, she finally managed to move her paws again. She turned and raced down the street, darting as quickly as she could past lamp-posts and parked cars. Behind her, she could hear the Alsatian barking noisily, and the man yelling for him to stop.

I've got to hide! Kitty thought desperately, picturing those horrible sharp teeth. She took the next left and ran up a steep hill. It was only when she was halfway up it, dodging past tangled weeds and patches of nettles, that she realised she was heading straight towards Mrs Thornton's house. The cracked dark windows and shabby front door came into view, and as Kitty ducked under the garden fence, hoping that the dog wouldn't be able to squeeze his body through it, she almost ran headfirst into another cat – Shadow! He yowled in surprise.

'What are you doing here again?' he miaowed. 'And what's all that noise?'

'I'm really sorry, I didn't mean to startle you!' panted Kitty. 'But I was running away from –'

Before she could finish, the Alsatian charged up the hill after Kitty. He growled noisily as he reached the fence and spotted not one, but *two* cats on the other side. He ran from one end of the fence to the other, barking in frustration as he scrabbled at the wood and searched for a way into the garden.

Shadow hissed, arching his back and tail, and both cats took several quick steps back. Kitty couldn't help trembling in fright.

'That nasty dog's going to wake up my human with all his barking!' Shadow said anxiously.

'Sorry, Shadow,' Kitty whispered.

'He just chased me up here. Look, his human's here now. I really hope he can get hold of him!' She'd never run into a dog in her cat form – it was petrifying!

'Nipper!' she heard the young man shout. 'Come here! Bad dog! No treats for you tonight!'

As the man tried to grab hold of his dog's lead, the Alsatian continued to jump against the fence. Suddenly Kitty found herself giving a terrified squeal – the dog had managed to push through one of the wooden posts and leap through the gap into the garden!

'Nipper, no!' shouted the young man, as the dog ran straight for Kitty. She turned and raced towards the nearest tree, pouncing up the trunk and shaking in the highest branches. The Alsatian tried to jump up after her, but he was much too heavy – so instead, he turned and fixed his gaze on Shadow!

At last, the man managed to grab hold of his dog's lead and wrap it firmly around his hand three times. 'Got you!' he said, sounding very relieved. 'We're going straight home. Bad dog!' With a jerk on the lead, he led the Alsatian out of Mrs Thornton's garden and down the hill.

Kitty felt herself slowly start to relax. The arch in her back began to drop, and the horrid pricking feeling in her fur started to disappear. She peered down through the leaves from the branch she was perched on. Shadow called up to her. 'Kitty, you can come down now!' he miaowed. 'That horrible dog and his human have gone.'

Kitty tried to find her footing to make her way down from the tree, but suddenly she felt unsure. 'I-I don't think I can come down, Shadow!' she called. 'I've never climbed this high up in a tree before. I think I'm stuck!' She looked down helplessly at the older black cat, starting to feel frightened again.

'It's OK, Kitty,' Shadow said, his miaow sounding more reassuring now. 'I'll help you climb down. I go up into that tree all the time!'

Kitty was grateful that Shadow was there to help her, but she felt bad – as the Guardian, her hope had been to help *him*!

'Now, you see that branch a little way below you, off to the right?' Shadow asked, sitting under the tree and looking up at Kitty. Kitty nodded, a bit too scared to miaow back. 'Shuffle backwards a bit towards the tree trunk, then jump down on to that branch. I promise, it's nice and strong. Use your tail for balance,' Shadow called.

Kitty took a deep breath, and then did as he'd explained. She made it!

'Well done, Kitty!' Shadow said. 'Now, just one more branch – can you see the one just below you? I left my claw marks on it a long time ago, so that I know which branch to use when I climb down. Jump on to there, and then you'll be able to make the leap down to the ground easily.'

'I'm not sure …' Kitty began. The ground still seemed so far away.

Shadow let out an encouraging purr.
'You can do it!'
Kitty swallowed, then jumped down

again on the branch Shadow had scratched. He was right! Now the ground seemed much closer. With a little miaow, she made the next jump, and was relieved to feel the grass under her paws again.

'Thank you so much, Shadow!' Kitty said with a relieved purr, bumping heads happily with the older cat without even thinking. Shadow seemed to hesitate a moment, but then returned her head bump too.

'That's OK,' he said.

Suddenly, an eerie-sounding creak came from behind her. Oh no! Even though things were a bit friendlier with Shadow now, Kitty couldn't help being worried about Mrs Thornton catching her in the garden. What if she was as scary as the kids at school said? Should she run away? But then what would Shadow think? They'd only just begun to make friends, and Kitty still wanted to help him if she could. Planting her paws and trying to be brave, Kitty watched as the front door of the spooky old house began to open …

Chapter 6

Kitty felt her whiskers tremble nervously. She knew deep down that the spooky rumours about Mrs Thornton were just silly stories – there was no such thing as *real* witches, after all. Even so, she was a bit worried.

Kitty held her breath as a frail, shaky voice called out, 'Shadow? Shadow, sweetheart!' Then a figure appeared on the front step and peered into the garden. Mrs Thornton had curly white hair, wore glasses on a long gold chain around her neck, and held a walking stick in front of her. She was surprisingly small, and moved very slowly.

'There you are, sweetheart,' she said, sounding relieved as Shadow trotted quickly over to her. He purred loudly, rubbing himself against her ankles. Kitty couldn't help feeling happy – and a bit jealous, like she did with Misty – about how much Shadow obviously loved his human. Mrs Thornton clearly loved Shadow too. She smiled happily, and bent down gingerly to scratch the soft fur under his chin, leaning heavily on her walking stick. 'You like that, don't you, sweetheart,' she said, and Shadow purred even louder, rolling on to his back as Mrs Thornton laughed. But then she noticed Kitty.

'Oh, who's this?' asked Mrs Thornton, reaching to put on her glasses and smiling. 'You've met another cat, have you, Shadow?'

Kitty stepped forward cautiously.

'It's OK, lovely!' She made kissing noises, and Kitty came closer. Mrs Thornton bent down to rub Kitty's head too, and Kitty gave a happy purr of her own. 'What a sweet little thing.' She looked around the garden. 'I thought I heard barking out here,' she said. 'I hope you two are all right. It's nice that you have a new friend, Shadow.

I can't remember the last time someone came to visit.'

She straightened up from stroking Kitty, and looked around with a sad expression on her face. 'Maybe it's for the best. I'm rather embarrassed at how untidy my garden looks. It wasn't always like this, full of horrid weeds and brambles, was it? You used to lie out in the sun while I gardened, didn't you, sweetheart?'

Shadow wound around her ankles again as she spoke. Kitty could tell he was hoping to cheer her up, but Mrs Thornton sighed and finally murmured, 'I just can't manage it since I fell and hurt my leg.'

She smiled down at Shadow. 'Never

mind, eh? I'm going back inside,
darling,' Mrs Thornton said, and then
turned back to Kitty. 'You're welcome
back whenever you like, little one!'

Kitty purred again. She was no longer afraid of Mrs Thornton's house. Now that she had met the old lady, and seen how friendly she really was, it didn't feel spooky any more. But she knew she had to get home, or Grandma would start to worry. Mrs Thornton went inside, leaving Shadow and Kitty alone in the garden.

'Your human is so lovely!' Kitty miaowed happily to Shadow.

'She's the best,' Shadow agreed shyly. 'I've been very worried about her lately. I haven't wanted to leave her alone since she had her fall, even though I've been so lonely here without any cats to play with.'

Kitty saw how sad Shadow was. 'Let

me help you!' she said. 'I'm the Guardian now and I'm sure –'

'There's nothing you can do,' Shadow interrupted gloomily before disappearing into the house, his tail drooping sadly behind him.

With Shadow gone, Kitty made her way home quickly.

When Kitty trotted into the living room, Grandma was sipping a cup of green tea and reading a book. She looked up with a smile. 'Hello there, Kitty cat!'

Kitty miaowed the words to change back into her human form, knowing it was OK to do it in front of Grandma.

'Kitten paws to human toes,
Kitten whiskers, human nose.'

She closed her eyes as the tingling

sensation swept over her furry body, and soon enough, she was looking down at her two hands, two feet, and the summer dress she'd been wearing that day!

She turned to Grandma quickly. 'Guess what? I met Shadow, and Mrs Thornton!'

She explained what she'd learned about the old lady's hurt leg. 'I saw how much Shadow loves his human. I think he won't leave the house or garden because he's afraid she'll be left by herself and have another fall, but that just means he's lonely up there too.' She finished, 'I want to call another Cat Council for tomorrow evening. There has to be a way for us to help Shadow, *and* Mrs Thornton.'

Grandma smiled. 'I think that's a very good idea, Kitty,' she said. 'I'm very proud of you. You're proving to be such a good Guardian already!'

Before Kitty went to bed, she quickly changed back into her cat form and slipped out on to the main street again. She padded up to a fence post and used her claws to scratch the special triangle symbol into the wood, then rubbed her fur against it. She gave a loud miaow, so that any cats nearby would hear. Now the message would start to spread, and soon the rest of the cats in town would know that a meeting had been called for tomorrow night!

The next night Kitty waited until her parents were fast asleep before excitedly turning into her cat form. She leapt through the open bathroom window this time and landed with a soft thud on the roof of her parents' car. She trotted quickly along the street in the direction of the woods for the Cat Council meeting. Kitty couldn't wait to tell the other cats what she'd learned. Once everyone understood why Shadow had been behaving so strangely, she was sure they'd want to help him.

Soon Kitty was at the clearing, where the other cats of the Council were starting to gather. Once everyone was sitting in their places, and Tiger had led the cats in reciting the Miaow Vow, he nodded at Kitty.

Kitty padded right into the middle of the circle. 'Thank you all for coming,' she miaowed. 'I wanted to tell you all that I found out why Shadow has been acting so oddly recently.'

The other cats' ears pricked up

with curiosity as Kitty explained about Mrs Thornton's fall. 'Shadow and Mrs Thornton love each other very much,' she told them. 'Shadow's not really unfriendly – he just doesn't want to leave his garden because he wants to stay at home to protect his human.'

Around the circle, many furry heads were nodding. 'I can understand that!' purred a fluffy grey Persian with a sparkly collar. 'My human looks after me and gives me cuddles every day. I would want to look after her too, if she was in trouble.'

Some of the other cats began to look at one another guiltily.

'I think because I don't have a human of my own, it took me a while to realise it,' Kitty said. 'Shadow is a little bit grumpy, but he's really nice deep down. He's just so worried about keeping Mrs Thornton company, he's ended up all alone at the top of the hill.'

'Oh dear,' said Tiger, shaking his furry head. 'I suppose we might have had the wrong impression about Shadow after all. Maybe we should have tried harder to find out what was wrong.'

Pinky curled her skinny, long tail around her, and Kitty could tell she felt bad about Shadow too. 'Well done for finding out what happened, Kitty,' she miaowed. 'You're such a good Guardian!'

Grandma led the other cats in miaows of agreement.

'But how are we going to help Shadow, Kitty?' asked a plump tabby.

'If Shadow doesn't want to leave his garden to come to us,' said Kitty, 'then we'll go to him! We're going to pay him a visit, right now.'

A ripple of surprise went through the circle. 'To that scary house?' asked Poppy nervously, her blue eyes very wide.

'Don't worry. You'll see when we get there that it's not that scary at all!' Kitty reassured her. 'Come on – everyone follow me.'

If any human had happened to glance out of their window that night, they would have seen an unusual sight: a long line of cats marching one by one down the street! Kitty led them up the hill and into Mrs Thornton's tangled garden. 'Shadow?' she miaowed. 'It's me – Kitty! And I've brought lots of friends with me!'

At first, Shadow was a little startled by how many cats were strolling through his garden – but as they said hello, he began to bump heads with them, timidly at first, then growing more confident.

'This is fantastic!' he miaowed to Kitty, purring happily as he watched some of the cats begin to chase after insects and play-fight with one another.

Kitty and Misty decided to start a game of hide-and-seek, and Shadow quickly showed them all how many fun places there were to hide in the wild, overgrown garden.

'I've missed playing!' he miaowed cheerfully. 'I've been so worried about my human that I just haven't felt like it.'

Kitty bumped heads with Shadow. 'See?' she miaowed. 'You've got lots of friends here – you don't have to be lonely.

Just ask whenever you want someone to play with, OK? Or for anything!'

Shadow purred his agreement. 'Thank you, Kitty,' he said.

'And we promise not just to assume you want to be by yourself!' Kitty added. 'Now we just need to think of a way to help your human too. And I think I've got an idea …'

Chapter 7

The next morning, Kitty couldn't wait to get to school. 'Why are we rushing, Kitty?' asked her mum, chuckling as Kitty practically sprinted the last few steps into the playground. 'Do you have a lesson you're really excited about?'

'I just need to talk to Jenny. It's important!' explained Kitty, reaching up to kiss her mum goodbye. Then she caught sight of Jenny's blonde ponytail. 'Oh look, there she is! See you tonight, Mum!'

Kitty raced over to meet Jenny. 'Guess where I was last night!' she said.

Jenny guessed the cinema, the swimming pool and the ice rink, before giving up. 'I was at that house at the top of the hill – the one belonging to Mrs Thornton!' explained Kitty.

Jenny stared at her friend. 'But *why* would you go up there? It's so spooky!' she replied.

As the bell rang and the girls walked into their classroom together, Kitty told Jenny that she'd gone for a walk after tea, and noticed a cat stuck up a tree in Mrs Thornton's garden. She had already planned that part of the story, because she knew she couldn't tell Jenny the truth — that *she* had been the cat in the tree in Shadow's garden — without revealing her secret and losing her magic! 'I … um … got some help getting the cat down,' she continued, 'and I ended up meeting Mrs Thornton. She was a *really* nice lady. She seemed lonely, living up there all by herself. And she had a bad fall a few months ago, so that's why her house and garden look so wild and scary. It's because she can't look after them any more.'

'Oh no, that's so sad,' said Jenny, pulling a face. 'Kitty, I feel awful for saying her house was scary now.'

'Well, I've thought of a way we can help her!' Kitty replied. 'Remember Ms Brookes's special project? She said we had to come up with an idea that would help the community. What if our class went and tidied up Mrs Thornton's garden for her? We could pull up the weeds, sweep up the dead leaves and plant some lovely new flowers for her. Maybe some of the teachers or parents could mend her broken windows and give her front door a fresh coat of paint. I'm sure she'd love having visitors up there as well.'

Jenny's face lit up. 'Kitty, that's a brilliant idea!'

'Let's hope Ms Brookes likes it,' replied Kitty. 'Come on – let's go and ask her.'

One week later, Kitty grinned proudly as she led her class up the hill towards Mrs Thornton's house, clutching a tray of daffodil bulbs in one hand and a little trowel in the other.

Ms Brookes had *loved* Kitty's idea. In fact, she'd liked it so much that she had gone to pay Mrs Thornton a visit that very same day. Mrs Thornton had been delighted with Kitty's suggestion, and the next morning, Ms Brookes had something to tell the class. 'We've had some excellent ideas for this year's special community project, but I have chosen the winner!' she had said.

When she had explained what they were going to do, some of Kitty's class-mates had seemed a little nervous about visiting the house on the hill, and even frightened, until Kitty had told them all about Mrs Thornton and how kind she really was. She couldn't wait for them all to meet her themselves.

As she reached the top of the hill, Kitty saw Mrs Thornton waiting on the steps of her house, and waved. 'Hi, Mrs Thornton! We're here!' she called.

Mrs Thornton beamed at Kitty. 'This is just wonderful!' she said. 'I'm so thrilled to see you all. I've baked lots of biscuits and cupcakes to keep your strength up, and there's homemade lemonade too.'

'Wow, she *is* nice!' Jenny whispered to Kitty, smiling.

Ms Brookes split the class into groups: one to sweep leaves into piles, one to pull up weeds and one to plant seeds. Everyone got to work and Mrs Thornton walked around carefully to hand out treats and talk to each person.

As Kitty and Jenny scattered their seeds, Kitty felt something soft and warm brush against her ankle.

'Shadow!' she said, bending down to stroke him. Turning quickly to make sure Jenny wouldn't be able to hear her, she leaned a bit closer and whispered, 'It's lovely to come back and see you again. And you might see me later on – but I'll be on four paws instead of two feet!' She grinned as Shadow gave an eager miaow and purred. Although she couldn't understand what Shadow was saying, she could tell he was happy.

That night, Kitty returned to Mrs Thornton's house – just as she'd

promised Shadow – but this time she padded lightly up the hill in her cat form, with her tail waving behind her. Grandma ran next to her, and some of her cat friends followed: Misty, Tiger, Ruby and Bella. Everyone was curious to see what Kitty and her class had done!

'Kitty, it looks wonderful!' purred Grandma as the house and garden came into view. In the moonlight, the neat rows of flowers, plants and herbs were clear, and the grass on the lawn was neatly trimmed.

'It looks so different. Not spooky at all!' added Misty.

'My human loves it, and so do I!' piped up a happy voice nearby.

The cats turned to see Shadow – who was sitting *outside* the garden fence! 'Shadow, you're not staying inside your house or your garden any more!' miaowed Kitty.

Shadow padded forward to bump foreheads with Kitty and all the other cats. 'That's right! I don't need to be worried about my human. She made lots of new friends today. And I've made lots of new friends too!' he added, purring shyly.

Grandma gave Kitty a nudge with her nose. 'Well done, Kitty!' she whispered. 'I'm so proud of you. Being brave and kind and friendly are all very important parts of being a Guardian, and I can see from how well you've helped Shadow that you're good at all three of those things!'

Kitty purred happily. 'Thank you, Grandma,' she whispered back. 'I love all the things I'm learning about being the Guardian. And most of all? I love, love, *love* being a cat!'

Kitty's best friend has
a brand new kitten!

But Misty is too
scared to go outside.

Can Kitty use her magic and
help Misty to be braver?

Turn over to read some of
Kitty's first ever adventure...

Kitty's magic

Misty the Scared Kitten

Chapter 1

'Grandma! Grandma!' shouted Kitty Kimura excitedly. 'A postcard's arrived from Mum and Dad!'

Kitty ran to the kitchen. Emails were nice, but she loved getting post! The card had a picture of a waving ceramic cat on it. In Japan, they were a sign of good luck. Her parents were in Japan again now.

Grandma was pouring tea into her

flowery cup. She smiled as Kitty read the short message aloud and then stuck the postcard on the fridge.

Kitty's grandma had been born in Japan, but moved to England when Kitty's dad was little. Kitty's parents now owned a shop that sold special Japanese things, and Kitty loved all the silky kimonos, colourful fans and sparkly mobile phone charms. Three times a year, her parents went to Tokyo to look for new things for the shop.

Grandma lived with Kitty and her parents, so they spent lots of time together, especially when Mum and Dad were away. Kitty missed them, but she loved being with Grandma. They even looked alike, with the same almond-shaped eyes. But Kitty's hair was long and black, while Grandma's bob had a streak of pure white on one side of her fringe.

'What shall we do for the rest of the week, Kitty-cat?' Grandma said.

Kitty's real name was Koemi, but she loved cats so much that she was given the nickname Kitty, and now everyone called her that!

Just as Kitty was about to answer, the phone rang.

'I'll get it,' Kitty offered, running into the living room.

She picked up the phone. 'Hello?'

'Kitty!' said an eager voice. 'It's me, Jenny!'

Kitty was surprised. Jenny was her

best friend, but they hardly ever phoned each other, because Jenny only lived three houses away. 'Hi!' she replied.

'Can you come to my house for a sleep-over tonight?' Jenny burst out. 'I have something really exciting to show you!'

Kitty giggled. Jenny was always

cheerful, but today she sounded even happier than usual. 'What is it?' she asked.

Jenny paused for a second. 'Well … I was going to keep it a surprise until you got here, but I can't wait. I've got a kitten!'

Kitty gasped. 'Jenny, you're so lucky!' she said, a smile spreading over her face. 'Why didn't you tell me before?'

'I didn't know until today!' Jenny explained. Kitty could hear her friend bouncing up and down excitedly. 'Mum kept it a surprise until I got home from school. My Auntie Megan is moving to America and she couldn't take her kitten with her – so she's given Misty to me! Wait till you see her, Kitty. She's gorgeous. She's pale grey with darker grey stripes. Mum says she's a silver tabby. And I think she likes me already. As soon as Auntie Megan brought her over, she ran straight up to me and rubbed herself all around my ankles!'

'I can't believe it,' Kitty said wistfully. 'I *love* cats.'

'I know! That's why I rang you straight away,' Jenny replied. 'It'll be as if she's your cat too! So can you come? We can play with Misty all evening!'

'Let me ask Grandma,' Kitty told her friend. 'I'll call you right back!'

She put down the phone and raced back into the kitchen. 'Grandma!' she called breathlessly. 'Can I sleep over at Jenny's house tonight? She's just got a *kitten*!'

Grandma put down her teacup. 'A kitten?' she replied slowly. 'Well, that's lovely for Jenny ... but, Kitty, you know you start to sneeze as soon as you're anywhere near a cat.'

Kitty bit her lip. It was true. Ever since she was a baby she had been allergic to cats. It made her feel sad and a bit cross, because cats were her favourite animals in the whole world. She loved their bright eyes, their silky fur, and the soft rumble of their purring.

Most of all, she liked imagining what the cats in her village got up to at night, when people were fast asleep! What made it even harder was that cats seemed to really like *her*, too. They always followed her down the street, rubbing their soft heads against her ankles and miaowing eagerly. Kitty couldn't resist bending down to stroke them, but she always ended up with sore eyes and a runny nose.

'Oh, please, Grandma,' she begged. 'I'll take lots of tissues, and if I start to get itchy eyes or a tickly nose, I'll stop playing with Misty straight away, I promise.'

Grandma gazed thoughtfully at Kitty. 'Well, maybe you are old enough now,' she murmured softly, with the hint of a smile on her lips.

'What do you mean, Grandma?' asked Kitty, frowning. *Old enough that my allergy will be gone?* she thought, confused.

'Never mind,' Grandma told her, shaking her head. 'Wait here, sweetheart. I have something for you.'

Kitty bit her lip, curious. Grandma sometimes acted a bit strangely. She often took long naps at funny times, and she would stay up late, saying she was watching her favourite TV programmes. But now she was behaving even more oddly than normal.

When Grandma came back, she placed something carefully into Kitty's hands. It was a slim silver chain with a small charm hanging from it. At first Kitty thought there were Japanese symbols on it. But as she looked more closely, she saw it was a tiny picture of a cat.

'Wow,' breathed Kitty, slipping the necklace over her head. 'It's beautiful.'

Grandma smiled and reached under her blue silk scarf to show Kitty a matching necklace. 'I have one too,' she explained. 'They have been in our family for a long time. Yours belonged to your great-grandmother. I've been keeping it safe until the right moment. It's very precious, and I know you will take good care of it. Make sure you wear it at Jenny's house. I think it will help with your allergies.'

'You mean ... I'm allowed to go?' cried Kitty. 'Thank you, Grandma!'

Kitty flung her arms around Grandma, though she was puzzled about what she'd said about the necklace. How could a piece of jewellery stop her from sneezing? But she was too excited to ask questions. She was going for a sleepover at her best friend's house, and she was going to play with a sweet little kitten!

Chapter 2

Half an hour later, Kitty and Grandma set off for Jenny's house, swinging Kitty's overnight bag between them. As soon as Kitty pressed the doorbell, the door burst open. Jenny's freckled face was flushed pink with excitement. 'I couldn't wait for you to get here!' she said with a grin. 'Quick – come and meet Misty!'

Jenny led them into the kitchen, where Jenny's mum and little brother Barney were painting. Jenny's mum washed her hands and made a cup of tea for Grandma. Kitty looked around eagerly for Misty. 'Where is she?'

'Over there, on the window sill!' said Jenny.

Kitty gasped as she spotted the little cat. 'Oh, she's *so cute*!' she cried.

Misty was curled cosily in a beam of warm sunshine. She was a soft grey colour, with darker grey stripes all over her body, and long silver whiskers. Her eyes were a pretty blue. When she spotted the girls, she sat straight up with pricked ears and gave a happy mew.

MEET

Kitty

Kitty is a little girl who can magically turn into a cat! She is the Guardian of the Cat Council

Tiger

Tiger is a big, brave tabby tom-cat. He is leader of the Cat Council

Suki

Suki is Kitty's grandmother. She can magically turn into a cat too!

THE CATS

Shadow

Shadow can be very shy with new cats. He is amazing at climbing trees

Pinky

Pinky is a very rare breed of cat without any hair at all! She is wise and friendly

Bella

Bella is an excitable kitten! Her coat is made up of many different colours

FELINE FACTS

Here are some
fun facts about our
purrrfect animal friends
that you might like
to know ...

1.

Cats close their
eyes when they
are **happy**

2.

Cats can't taste
sweet things

3.

Every cat's nose
is as unique as a
fingerprint

4.

Cats **always**
land on their feet

5.

Cats can make over
one hundred
different sounds

HtjaMogütáT